There Was an Old Lady
Who Swallowed a Trout!

for Betty Huffmon and for my daughter, Becky
—T. S.

for Rebecca, Alex, Ranger, Seth, and Theo
—R. R.

Henry Holt and Company, LLC, *Publishers since 1866*,
175 Fifth Avenue, New York, New York 10010
www.henryholtchildrensbooks.com

Library of Congress Cataloging-in-Publication Data
Sloat, Teri. There was an old lady who swallowed a trout / text by Teri Sloat ;
illustrations by Reynold Ruffins. Summary : Set on the coast of the Pacific Northwest,
this variation on the traditional cumulative rhyme describes the silly consequences
of an old woman's fishy diet. [1. Marine animals—Fiction. 2. Northwest, Pacific—Fiction.
3. Nonsense verses.] I. Ruffins, Reynold, ill. II. Title. PZ8.3.S63316Th 1998 [E]—dc21 98-11607

ISBN-13 : 978-0-8050-4294-8 / ISBN-10 : 0-8050-4294-6 (hardcover)
9 11 13 15 14 12 10 8

ISBN-13 : 978-0-8050-6900-6 / ISBN-10 : 0-8050-6900-3 (paperback)
7 9 10 8 6

First published in hardcover in 1998 by Henry Holt and Company
First paperback edition—2002
Typography by Meredith Baldwin
Printed in China on acid-free paper. ∞

There Was an Old Lady
Who Swallowed a Trout!

Teri Sloat
illustrated by Reynold Ruffins

Henry Holt and Company • New York

There was an old lady who swallowed a trout
That splished and splashed and thrashed about.

It wanted *out!*

There was an old lady who swallowed a salmon
That slippity-flippity-flopped as it swam in.

She swallowed the salmon to catch the trout

That splished and splashed
and thrashed about.
It wanted *out!*

There was an old lady who swallowed an otter.
With a mug of clear water, she swallowed the otter.

She swallowed the otter to catch the salmon;
She swallowed the salmon to catch the trout
That splished and splashed and thrashed about.

It wanted *out!*

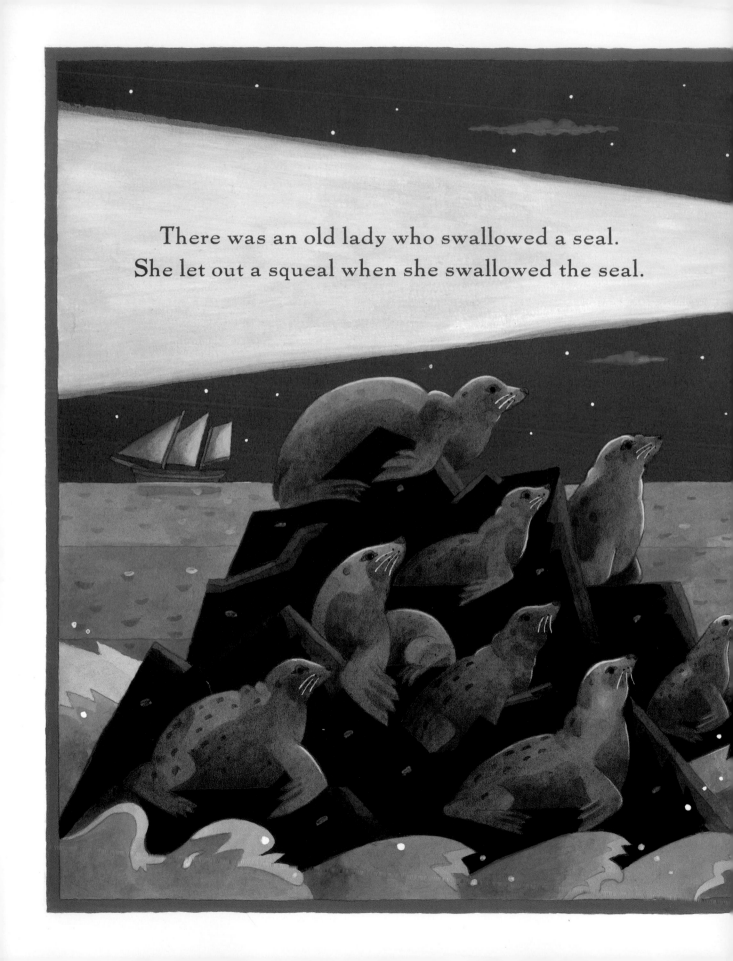

There was an old lady who swallowed a seal.
She let out a squeal when she swallowed the seal.

She swallowed the seal to catch the otter;
She swallowed the otter to catch the salmon;
She swallowed the salmon to catch the trout
That splished and splashed and thrashed about.

It wanted *out!*

There was an old lady who swallowed a porpoise.

She did it on purpose; she swallowed the porpoise.

She swallowed the porpoise to catch the seal;
She swallowed the seal to catch the otter;
She swallowed the otter to catch the salmon;
She swallowed the salmon to catch the trout
That splished and splashed and thrashed about.

It wanted *out!*

There was an old lady who swallowed a walrus.
With a great deal of fuss, she swallowed the walrus.

She swallowed the walrus to catch the porpoise;
She swallowed the porpoise to catch the seal;
She swallowed the seal to catch the otter;
She swallowed the otter to catch the salmon;
She swallowed the salmon to catch the trout
That splished and splashed and thrashed about.

It wanted *out!*

There was an old lady who swallowed a whale.
From its tip to its tail, she swallowed that whale.

She swallowed the whale to catch the walrus;
She swallowed the walrus to catch the porpoise;
She swallowed the porpoise to catch the seal;
She swallowed the seal to catch the otter;
She swallowed the otter to catch the salmon;
She swallowed the salmon to catch the trout
That splished and splashed and thrashed about.

It wanted *out!*

There was an old lady who swallowed the ocean.
What a commotion! She swallowed the ocean!

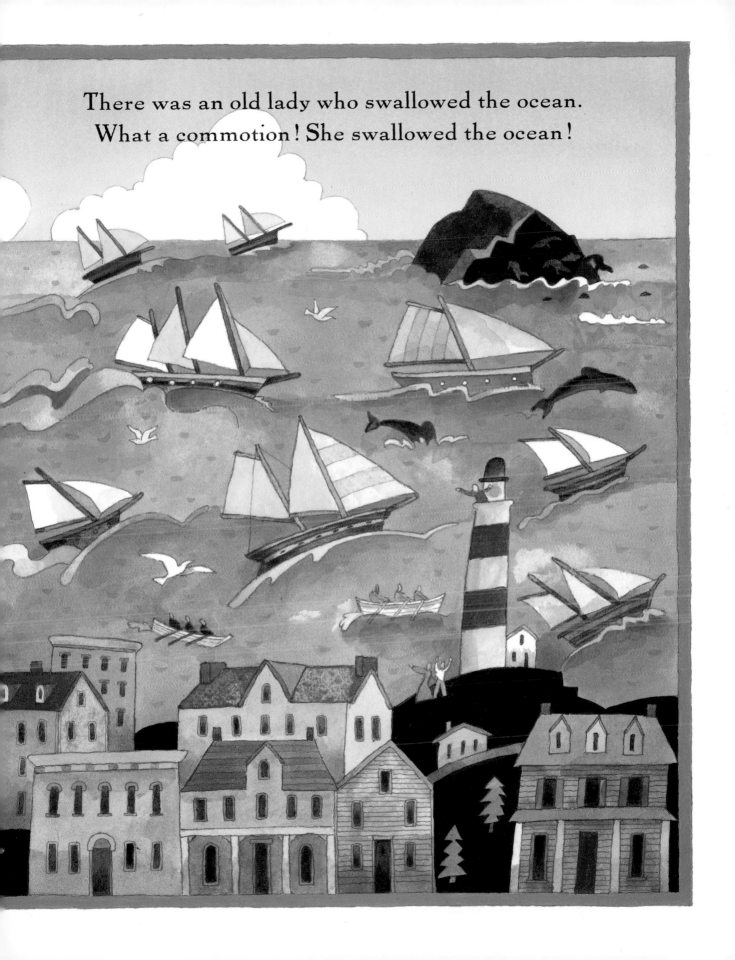

She swallowed the ocean to hold the whale
That now had plenty of room for its tail.
She swallowed the whale to catch the walrus;
She swallowed the walrus to catch the porpoise;
She swallowed the porpoise to catch the seal;
She swallowed the seal to catch the otter;
She swallowed the otter to catch the salmon;
She swallowed the salmon to catch the trout
That splished and splashed and thrashed about.

It wanted *out!*

The old lady started to wriggle and jiggle;
The swirling inside made her hiccup and giggle.
It made her laugh; it made her shout,
And when the old lady opened her mouth . . .

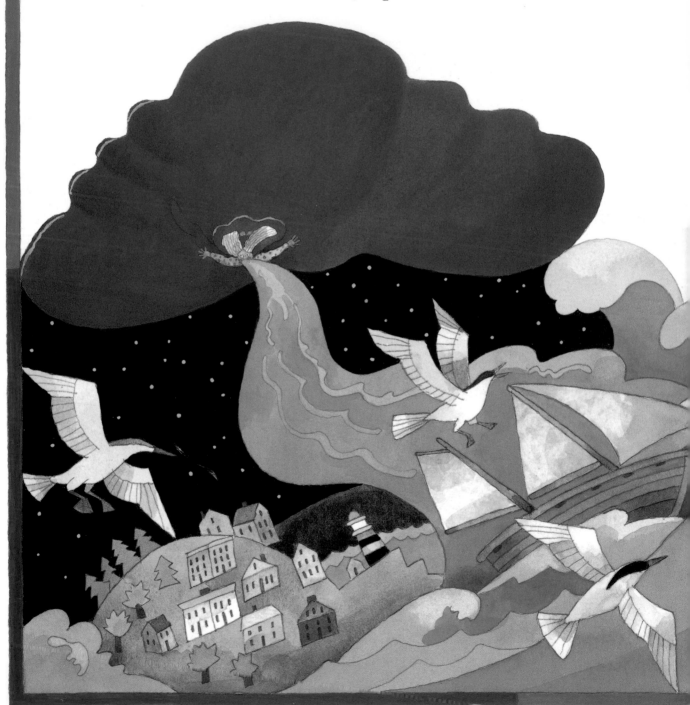

She let out the ocean, the whale, and the walrus,
She let out the porpoise she'd swallowed on purpose;
The seal, the otter, the salmon and trout,
Splished and splashed and thrashed about,

And they all swam

OUT!

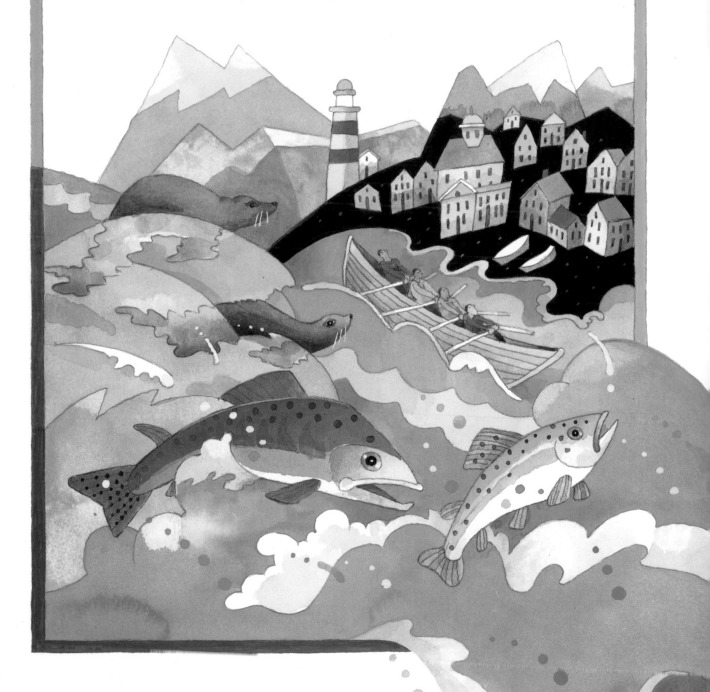